GOLDI ROCKS and the THREE BEARS

by **Corey Rosen Schwartz**
and **Beth Coulton**
illustrated by **Nate Wragg**

G. P. PUTNAM'S SONS

An Imprint of Penguin Group (USA)

To my mom and dad, for helping me wrestle
with the rhymes until they were "just right."
—C.R.S.

To my husband, Steve,
and my children, Chris, Lauren and Spencer—
my biggest fans and encouragers!
—B.C.

For my wife, Crystal, and my daughter, Willow—
you are my everlasting source of joy and inspiration.
—N.W.

G. P. PUTNAM'S SONS
Published by the Penguin Group
Penguin Group (USA) LLC
375 Hudson Street
New York, NY 10014

USA | Canada | UK | Ireland | Australia | New Zealand | India | South Africa | China
penguin.com
A Penguin Random House Company

Library of Congress Cataloging-in-Publication Data
Schwartz, Corey Rosen, author.
Goldi Rocks and the three bears / by Corey Rosen Schwartz and Beth Coulton ; illustrated by Nate Wragg.
pages cm
Summary: In this fractured fairy tale, the Three Bear Band holds tryouts for a lead singer.
[1. Stories in rhyme. 2. Rock groups—Fiction. 3. Bears—Fiction.] I. Coulton, Beth, author. II. Wragg, Nate, illustrator. III. Title.
PZ8.3.S29746Go 2014
[E]—dc23
2012046278
Manufactured in China by South China Printing Co. Ltd.
ISBN 978-0-399-25685-1
1 3 5 7 9 10 8 6 4 2

Design by Annie Ericsson.
Text set in Montara Gothic.
The art was done with pencil, painted textures, and Adobe Photoshop.

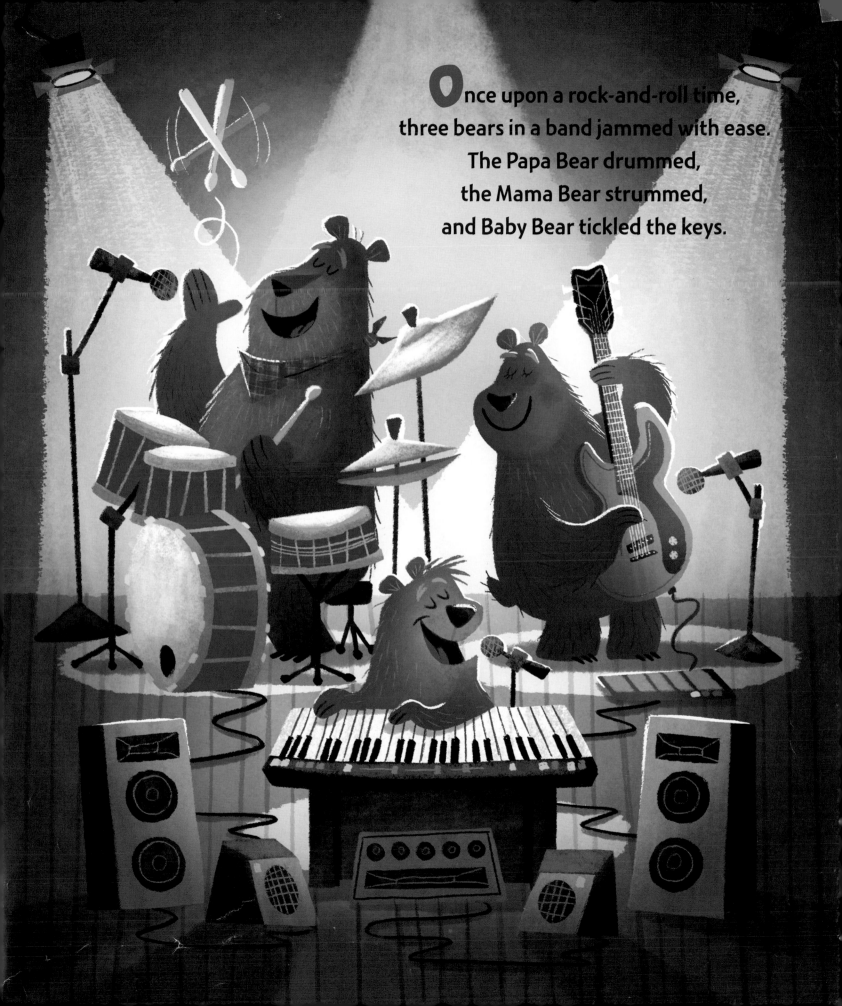

Once upon a rock-and-roll time,
three bears in a band jammed with ease.
The Papa Bear drummed,
the Mama Bear strummed,
and Baby Bear tickled the keys.

But the band didn't have many fans yet,
and Papa Bear figured out why . . .

"Though we all love to croon
and can carry a tune,
we can't hit the notes
way up high."

So they set out to find a soprano.
Soon after they left, a girl knocked.

"Is that porridge I smell?
Gee, that would be swell."
She checked, and the house was unlocked.

"A studio! Great balls of fire!"
Amazed, Goldi raced through the door.
She forgot about food
and was now in the mood
to hurry on in and explore.

The Mama Bear's mike hit her elbow,
and Pop's reached the top of her head.

But Baby's was hiked
to just where she liked.
"I'll give it a whirl," Goldi said.

She grabbed it and started performing.
"Oh dooby wop, dum diddy doo."

She was singing quite well
till she stumbled and fell
and the microphone stand broke in two.

So Goldi said, "I'll try the headphones."
But Mama Bear's pair was too tight.
The Papa's were loose.
"Gee, these are no use."
But Baby Bear's fit her just right.

That tune was so catchy, thought Goldi.
I'd love to be part of their band.
The guitar was too twangy.
The cymbals too clangy.
The piano was perfectly grand.

Exhausted from moving and grooving,
she needed to catch a few Z's.
"This day's been a doozy!
I'm feeling quite snoozy."
She dozed off on Baby Bear's keys.

In the meantime,
the Bears had held tryouts,
but no one had blown them away.

The hare was too twitchy.
The pigs were too pitchy.

And Red was just simply "okay."

The family returned to their cottage,
distressed from their lack of success.
When they saw the inside,
the Mama Bear cried,
"Egads! What a terrible mess!"

"Someone's been using my mike stand."
"Someone's been using mine, too."
Then Baby Bear spoke:
"Oh, no! My stand broke!"
He started to sniffle. "Boo-hoo!"

Then Mama Bear looked at her headphones.
"Oh, someone has tried my pair on!"
"Mine too," Papa growled.
The parents both scowled

Then Papa said,
"Who played my drum set?"
And Mama said,
"Who plucked my strings?"
"Well, who's in my chair?"
asked the littlest bear.
"She's drooling all over my things!"

They stared at the slumbering blond girl, and Papa asked, "Who could she BE?"

He disrupted her dream.
She awoke with a scream—
the pitch was a perfect high C!

The Bears asked to hear a whole medley
once Goldi recovered from shock.
"Amazing," said Mom.
Pop grinned. "You're the bomb."
And Baby cried, "Goldi can rock!"

Together they wrote a new ditty.
They practiced it into the night.
And soon their new jingle
became a hit single—
"Too Hot, Too Cold, or Just Right?"

Their albums now top all the rock charts.
A countrywide tour has been planned.
The fans scream and shout.
They're crazy about . . .